CONTENTS

FOREWORD

When I was small I loved the bits of *Alice* that I could understand, although I found the book difficult to read. Its difficulty puzzled me because I was told it was a children's story and I was a child. The bits I liked were the jokes and the characters, but I was not drawn to the pictures. As I got older, I understood the delicate threads of the book better and I was able to see the brilliance of Tenniel's illustrations, although I still wished I had been able to make sense of the nonsense when I was young. Then, years later, I could not resist trying to present these madcap characters in a different way, a way that I felt would be more accessible to children *now* – children with different tastes and outlooks from those of a hundred and fifty years ago.

When I first approached the story, I was not concerned with the classic, but rather with the timeless children's stories that I had come to love. (Does timeless mean that children have no time? If only we could ask the Mad Hatter!) So I cut

LEWIS CARROLL

Alice's

es in

land

RATED BY

Tony Ross

ANDERSEN PRESS

a lot from the text in terms of words, but I have tried not to cut the meaning and of course have drawn a lot of new pictures. I hope that in doing this I have made these wonderful adventures a little easier for young children – something that Lewis Carroll wanted to do when he did his own nursery edition "to be thumbed, to be cooed over..." The most important thing I have tried to do though has been to retain the spirit of the original so I must ask you to read the book and in the words of the King, "Consider your verdict," although as the Rabbit interrupted, "Not yet! There's a great deal to come before that..."

Tony Ross

Eastertide, 1993

CHAPTER 1
Down the Rabbit-hole

Alice was beginning to get very tired of sitting by her sister on the bank, and having nothing to do. She was considering (as well as she could, for the hot day made her feel very sleepy) whether making a daisy chain would be worth the trouble, when suddenly a White Rabbit with pink eyes ran by.

Alice found nothing remarkable in that, nor to hear the Rabbit say to itself, "Oh dear! Oh dear! I shall be too late!", but when it actually took a watch out of its waistcoat pocket and looked at it, she started to her feet, burning with curiosity. She ran across the field after it, just in time to see it pop down a large rabbit-hole under the hedge.

Down went Alice after it, never thinking how she was to get out again. The rabbit-hole went straight on for some way, and then dipped down so suddenly that Alice found herself falling down a deep well.

She fell very slowly, so she had plenty of time to look around her. The sides of the well were filled with cupboards and bookshelves; here and there maps and pictures hung on pegs.

Down, down, down.

Would the fall never end? "I wonder how many miles I've fallen?" she said aloud. "I must be getting near the centre of the earth. I wonder if I shall fall right through! How funny it'll seem to come out among the people that walk with their heads downwards. I shall have to ask them, 'Please, is this New Zealand or Australia?'"

Down, down, down.

As there was nothing else to do, Alice continued talking. "I expect Dinah'll miss me tonight." (Dinah was the cat.) "Dinah, my dear, I wish you were with me. There are no mice, I'm afraid, but you might catch a bat." Alice began to get rather sleepy, and went on, "Do cats eat bats? Do bats eat cats?"

She was just dozing off, when she landed with a thump on a heap of dry leaves. The fall was over. Before her was another long passage, with the White Rabbit still in sight, hurrying down it. Away went Alice, just in time to hear it say, "Oh my ears and whiskers, how late it's getting!"

She turned a corner, to find herself in a long, low hall, lit by lamps hanging from the roof. The White Rabbit was nowhere to be seen. There were doors all round the hall, but they were locked, and Alice walked sadly down the middle, wondering how she was ever to get out again.

Suddenly she came upon a little three-legged table, made of glass; on it there was a tiny golden key. Alice's first thought was that it might belong to one of the doors of the hall, but it was too small. However, behind a curtain was a little door about fifteen inches high: she tried the key in the lock, and to her delight it fitted.

The door led to a small passage, not much larger than a rat-hole; she looked along the passage into the loveliest garden. How she longed to wander among the bright flowers and cool fountains! But she could not even get her head through the doorway.

There seemed no use in trying, so she went back to the table, half hoping to find another key. This time, there was a little bottle on it, and round its neck a paper label with 'DRINK ME' beautifully printed on it in large letters.

It was all very well to say 'Drink me', but Alice was not going to do that in a hurry. "No, I'll look first," she said, "and see whether it's marked 'poison' or not." For she had read several stories about children who had not been careful; and if you drink from a bottle marked 'poison', it is certain to disagree with you, sooner or later. However, this bottle was not marked 'poison', so Alice tasted it, and finding it very nice (it had a sort of mixed flavour of custard and turkey), she finished it off.

"What a curious feeling!" said Alice. "I must be shutting up like a telescope."

And so it was. She was now only ten inches high, just the right size for going through the little door. When she got to the door, though, she found that she had forgotten the little key, and when she went back to the table for it, she could see it through the glass, but she could not possibly reach it.

She tried to climb up one of the table legs but it was too slippery; and when she had tired herself out with trying, she sat down and began to cry.

Suddenly, her eye fell on a little glass box, lying under the table; she opened it, and found a small cake with the words

beautifully marked in currants. "Well, I'll eat it," said Alice, "and if it makes me larger, I can reach the key, and if it makes me smaller, I can creep under the door; so either way, I'll get into the garden."

She ate a little bit, and was quite surprised to find that she remained the same size; so she finished the cake.

CHAPTER 2
The Pool of Tears

"Curioser and curioser!" cried Alice. (She was so surprised, she quite forgot to speak good English.) "Now I'm opening up like a telescope! Goodbye, feet!" (When she looked down at her feet, they seemed to be almost out of sight.) "I wonder who will put on your shoes for you now. You must manage the best way you can."

Just then, her head struck the roof of the hall. She was now more than nine feet high, and she again took the golden key and hurried off to the garden door.

Poor Alice! It was as much as she could do, lying down, to look into the garden; to get through was hopeless. She sat down and began to cry again.

"You ought to be ashamed of yourself," she said, "to go on crying this way! Stop this moment!" But she went on, shedding gallons of tears, until there was a large pool all round her, about four inches deep and reaching halfway down the hall.

After a time, she heard a pattering of feet in the distance. It was the White Rabbit, with a pair of kid gloves in one hand and a large fan in the other. He came trotting along, muttering to himself, "The Duchess, the Duchess! Oh! I've kept her waiting!"

Alice was ready to ask help from anyone, so she began, in a timid voice, "If you please, sir –"

The Rabbit started, dropped the gloves and fan, and scurried away into the darkness.

Alice picked up the fan and gloves, and, as the hall was hot, she kept fanning herself as she talked. "Dear, dear! How queer everything is today! I wonder if I've changed in the night? Who in the world am I?" And she began thinking of all the children she knew.

"I'm not Ada," she said, "her hair goes in ringlets, and mine doesn't, and I'm sure I can't be Mabel, for I know all sorts of things, and she knows very little. I'll see if I know the things I used to know. Let me see: four times five is twelve, and four times six is – oh dear! Let's try Geography. London is the capital of Paris, and Paris is the capital of Rome – no, that's wrong. I must have changed in to Mabel! I'll try and say 'How doth the little…'" She crossed her hands on her lap and began, but the words did not come out as they used to do:

"How doth the little crocodile
Improve his shining tail,
And pour the waters of the Nile
On every golden scale!

How cheerfully he seems to grin,
How neatly spreads his claws,
And welcomes little fishes in,
With gently smiling jaws!"

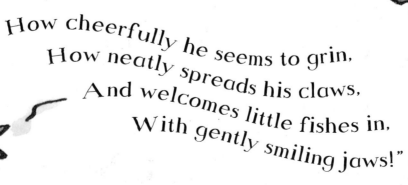

"I'm sure those are not the right words," said poor Alice, and her eyes filled with tears again. "I must be Mabel after all!"

As she said this, she was surprised to see that she had put on one of the Rabbit's gloves. "How can I have done that?" she thought. "I must be growing small again." She was now about two feet high, and was shrinking fast: she soon found out that the cause of this was the fan she was holding, and she dropped it, just in time to avoid shrinking away altogether.

"That was a narrow escape!" said Alice. "And now for the garden!" She ran back to the little door, but, alas! It was shut again, and the golden key was lying on the glass table as before. "And things are worse than ever," she thought, "for I was never this small before!"

As she spoke, her foot slipped, and splash! She was up to her chin in salt water. Her first idea was that somehow she was in the sea; however, she soon made out that she was in the pool of tears which she had wept when she was nine feet high.

"I wish I hadn't cried so much!" said Alice as she swam about, trying to find her way out. Just then, she heard something splashing about: at first she thought it must be a hippopotamus, but then remembered how small she was, and saw that it was only a mouse that had slipped in like herself.

"Would it be of any use," thought Alice, "to speak to this mouse?" So she began: "O Mouse, do you know the way out of this pool?"

The Mouse looked at her, and seemed to wink with one of its little eyes, but it said nothing.

"I daresay it's a French mouse, and doesn't understand English," thought Alice, so she began again: "*Où est ma chatte?*" which was the first sentence in her French lesson book.

The Mouse gave a sudden leap out of the water and quivered with fright.

"Oh, I beg your pardon!" cried Alice. "I forgot you didn't like cats."

"Not like cats!" cried the Mouse. "Would you like cats if you were me?"

"Well, perhaps not," said Alice in a soothing tone. "Yet I wish I could show you our cat Dinah. She is such a dear thing. She sits purring so nicely by the fire, and she's such a one for

catching mice – oh, I beg your pardon!" The Mouse was bristling all over. "We won't talk about her any more."

"We, indeed!" cried the Mouse, trembling to the end of its tail. "As if I would talk on such a subject. Our family has always hated cats, nasty vulgar things!"

Alice hurriedly changed the subject. "Are you fond of dogs? There is such a nice little dog near our house I should like to show you. A little bright-eyed terrier with long brown hair. It'll fetch things when you throw them. It belongs to a farmer who says it kills all the rats and – oh dear!"

The Mouse was swimming away from her as hard as it could.

"Do come back," she called after it, "and we won't talk about cats or dogs either."

When the Mouse heard this, it turned round and swam slowly back, and said in a trembling voice, "Let us get to the shore, and I'll tell you my history, and you'll understand why I hate cats and dogs."

It was high time to go, for the pool was getting crowded with the birds and animals that had fallen in. There was a Duck and a Dodo, a Lory and an Eaglet, and several other curious creatures. Alice led the way, and the whole party swam to the shore.

CHAPTER 3

A Caucus-race and a Long Tale

They were a queer-looking party, assembled on the bank, all dripping wet, cross, and uncomfortable.

The first question was how to get dry again. The Mouse, who seemed to be a person of authority, called out, "Sit down, all of you, and listen to me! I'll soon make you dry!" They all sat down in a large ring, with the Mouse in the middle.

"Ahem!" said the Mouse. "This is the driest thing I know. 'William the Conqueror was soon submitted to by the English, who wanted leaders–'"

"Ugh!" said the Lory, with a shiver.

"Pardon!" said the Mouse. "Did you speak?"

"No!" said the Lory hastily.

"I thought you did," said the Mouse. "I proceed. 'The Archbishop of Canterbury found it advisable – '"

"Found what?" said the Duck.

"Found it," the Mouse replied crossly, "you know what 'it' means."

"I know what 'it' means when I find something," said the Duck. "It's generally a frog or a worm. The question is, what did the Archbishop find?"

The Mouse ignored this, and went on, "' – found it advisable to offer William the crown.' How are you getting on now, my dear?" it continued, turning to Alice.

"As wet as ever," said Alice.

"In that case," said the Dodo, "I move that the meeting adjourn for the adoption of – "

"Speak English!" said the Eaglet. "I don't know the meaning of long words, and I don't believe you do either!"

"What I was going to say," said the Dodo, "was that the best thing to get us dry would be a Caucus-race."

"What is a Caucus-race?" said Alice; not that she much wanted to know.

"Why," said the Dodo, "the best way to explain it is to do it."

First it marked out a course in a circle ("the exact shape doesn't matter," it said), then everybody was placed round it, here and there. There was no start, but they began running when they liked, and stopped when they liked. After half an hour, they were all quite dry again, and the Dodo called out, "The race is over!" Everybody crowded round, panting, and asking, "Who has won?"

The Dodo said, "Everybody has won, and all must have prizes."

"But who will give the prizes?" a chorus of voices asked.

"Why, she, of course," said the Dodo, pointing at Alice.

Everybody crowded round her, calling, "Prizes, prizes!"

Alice had no idea what to do, so she pulled a bag of sweets from her pocket and handed them round.

"But you must have a prize yourself," said the Mouse. "What else have you got in your pocket?"

"Only a thimble," said Alice.

"Hand it over," said the Dodo, and everybody crowded round once more while the Dodo solemnly gave the thimble back to Alice.

They all looked so serious that Alice tried not to laugh. Instead, she said to the Mouse, "You promised to tell me your history, you know."

"Mine is a long and a sad tale!" said the Mouse, sighing.

"It is long," said Alice, looking at the Mouse's tail, "but why do you call it sad?" And she wondered about it while the Mouse was speaking, so that her idea of the tail was something like this:

"Fury said to a
mouse, that he
met in
the house,
'Let us both
go to law:
I will prosecute
you. Come,
I'll take
no denial:
we must
have the
trial;
for really this
morning I've
nothing
to do.'
Said the
mouse to
the cur,
'Such
a trial,
dear sir,
with no
Jury or
judge,
would be
wasting our
breath.'
'I'll be
judge,
I'll be
Jury,'
said
cunning
old
Fury:
'I'll try
the whole
cause,
and
condemn
you to
death.'"

"You are not listening!" said the Mouse, getting up and walking away.

"I'm sorry," said Alice. "Please come back and finish your story."

But the Mouse only shook its head, and walked a little quicker.

"What a pity it wouldn't stay!" said the Lory.

"I wish I had our Dinah here," said Alice. "She'd soon fetch it back!"

"And who is Dinah?" said the Lory.

"Our cat," replied Alice, "and she's a capital one for catching mice. And oh, you should see her after the birds! She'll eat a bird as soon as look at it."

This caused a sensation among the party. Some of the birds hurried off at once. One old magpie wrapped itself up, remarking, "I must be getting home; the night air doesn't suit my throat!"

Soon, Alice was left alone. "I wish I hadn't mentioned Dinah!" she said to herself, and she began to cry again, feeling very lonely.

In a while, however, she heard a pattering of feet, and she looked up, hoping it was the Mouse coming back to finish its story.

CHAPTER 4
The Rabbit Sends in a Little Bill

It was the White Rabbit, trotting slowly back again, and looking anxiously about. Alice heard it muttering, "The Duchess! The Duchess! Oh my fur and whiskers, she'll get me executed! Where can I have dropped them?"

Alice guessed that it was looking for the fan and the pair of gloves, which were nowhere to be seen.

Soon the Rabbit noticed Alice, and called out to her angrily, "Why, Mary Ann, what are you doing here? Run home this moment, and fetch me a pair of gloves and a fan! Quick, now!"

Alice was so frightened, she ran off in the direction it pointed to.

"He took me for his housemaid," she said to herself as she ran. "I'd better find him his fan and his gloves." As she said this, she came upon a neat little house, on the door of which was the name

'W. RABBIT'.

She went in without knocking, and hurried up the stairs. She found her way into a tidy little room with a table in the window, and on it, a fan and

two or three pairs of tiny white kid gloves. She took the fan and a pair of gloves, and was just about to leave, when her eye fell on a little bottle. There was no label saying 'DRINK ME', but she uncorked it and put it to her lips. "I know *something* interesting is sure to happen," she said to herself.

It did, and much sooner than she expected: before she had drunk half the bottle, she found her head pressing against the ceiling. She hastily put down the bottle, saying to herself, "That's quite enough. I can't get out at the door!" She went on growing, and soon had to lie down with one arm out of the window and one foot up the chimney.

Luckily for Alice, she grew no larger; still, it was very uncomfortable. "It was much pleasanter at home," thought poor Alice, "when I wasn't growing larger and smaller, and being ordered about by rabbits. I almost wish I hadn't gone down that rabbit-hole, and yet – "

"Mary Ann! Mary Ann!" said a voice. "Fetch me my gloves this moment!"

Alice knew it was the Rabbit, and she trembled, quite forgetting she was now a thousand times as large as it, with no reason to be afraid.

The Rabbit tried to open the door, but Alice's elbow was pressed against it, and that attempt was a failure. Then she heard the Rabbit just under the window. She suddenly spread out her hand and made a snatch in the air. There was a little shriek and a fall, and a crash of broken glass, from which she guessed it had fallen into a cucumber frame.

Next came an angry voice, the Rabbit's; "Pat, where are you?"

"I'm here!" said another voice. "Digging for apples, yer honour!"

"Digging for apples, indeed," said the Rabbit angrily. "Come and help me out of this!" (Sounds of more broken glass.) "Now tell me, Pat, what's that in the window?"

"It's an arm, yer honour."

"An arm, you goose! Whoever saw one that size? Take it away!"

Alice waited for some time without hearing anything more; at last came a rumbling of little cart-wheels, and the sound of many voices.

"Where's the other ladder?"

"Bill, fetch it here!"

"Tie 'em together first." "Will the roof hold?"

"Who's to go down the chimney?" "I won't!"

"Bill's to go down. Here, Bill!"

"Oh, so Bill's got to come down the chimney, has he?" said Alice to herself. "This fireplace is narrow, but I can kick a little!"

She waited till she heard a little animal scrambling about in the chimney, then, saying to herself, "This is Bill", she gave one sharp kick, and waited to see what would happen next. The first thing she heard was a chorus of "There goes Bill!"

Then silence, then another confusion of voices:
"Hold up his head." "Brandy now." "Don't choke him!" "How was it, old fellow?"

At last came a feeble squeak, "All I know is, something came at me, and up I goes like a sky-rocket."

"So you did!" said the others.

"We must burn the house down," said the Rabbit's voice.

Alice called out as loud as she could, "If you do, I'll set Dinah at you!"

There was a dead silence. After a minute or two, a shower of little pebbles came rattling in at the window, some of them hitting Alice in the face. She noticed with some surprise that the pebbles were turning into little cakes as they lay on the floor.

"If I eat one," she thought, "I'm sure to change size." So she swallowed one of the cakes, and was delighted to find that she began to

SHRink.

As soon as she was small enough, she ran out of the house, and found a crowd of little animals and birds waiting outside. The poor little lizard, Bill, was being held up by two guinea pigs, who were giving it something out of a bottle. They all made a rush at Alice, but she ran off as hard as she could, and soon found herself safe in a thick wood.

There was a large mushroom growing near her, about the same height as herself. When she stretched up and peeped over the edge of the mushroom, her eyes met those of a large blue caterpillar. It was sitting on the top, quietly smoking a hookah, and taking not the smallest notice of her or of anything else.

CHAPTER 5

Advice from a Caterpillar

The Caterpillar and Alice looked at each other for some time in silence. At last, the Caterpillar spoke.

"Who are you?" he said, in a sleepy voice.

"I hardly know, sir," said Alice. "I must have changed several times since I got up this morning. It's very confusing."

"It isn't," said the Caterpillar.

"Well, perhaps you haven't found it so yet," said Alice. "But when you have to turn into a butterfly, I think you'll feel a little queer."

"Not a bit," said the Caterpillar.

"It would feel very queer to me," said Alice.

"You!" said the Caterpillar with contempt. "Who are you?"

Alice felt irritated at this, and she said, "I think you should tell me who you are first."

"Why?" said the Caterpillar.

Alice could not think of any good reason.

The Caterpillar puffed away for some minutes without speaking. Then it unfolded its arms and said, "So you think you're changed?"

"I'm afraid I am, sir," said Alice. "I can't remember things

as I used to. I tried to say 'How doth the little busy bee', but it came out all different."

"Repeat 'You are old, Father William'," said the Caterpillar. Alice folded her hands, and began:

" 'You are old, Father William,' the young man said,
   'And your hair has become very white:
And yet you incessantly stand on your head -
   Do you think, at your age, it is right?'

'In my youth,' Father William replied to his son,
   'I feared it might injure the brain;
But, now that I'm perfectly sure I have none,
   Why, I do it again and again.'

'You are old,' said the youth, 'as I mentioned before,
   And have grown most uncommonly fat;
Yet you turned a back-somersault in at the door
   Pray, what is the reason of that?'

'In my youth,' said the sage, as he shook his grey locks,
   'I kept all my limbs very supple
By the use of this ointment - one shilling the box -
   Allow me to sell you a couple?'

'You are old,' said the youth, 'and your jaws are too weak
   For anything tougher than suet;
Yet you finished the goose, with the bones and the beak
   Pray, how did you manage to do it?'

'In my youth,' said his father, 'I took to the law,
   And argued each case with my wife;
And the muscular strength which it gave to my jaw,
   Has lasted the rest of my life.'

'You are old,' said the youth, 'one would hardly suppose
   That your eye was as steady as ever;
Yet you balanced an eel on the end of your nose
   What made you so awfully clever?'

'I have answered three questions, and that is enough,'
   Said his father; 'don't give yourself airs!
Do you think I can listen all day to such stuff?
   Be off, or I'll kick you down stairs!' "

"It's wrong from beginning to end," said the Caterpillar. There was another silence. "What size do you want to be?"

"I would like to be a little larger, sir," said Alice. "Three inches is such a wretched height to be."

"It is a very good height!" said the Caterpillar angrily, rearing itself upright (it was exactly three inches high).

"I wish the creatures wouldn't be so easily offended," Alice thought.

The Caterpillar yawned, got down off the mushroom, and crawled away into the grass. "One side will make you taller, the other side will make you shorter," it remarked. In a moment, it was out of sight.

Alice looked at the mushroom, trying to make out its sides, as it was perfectly round. She stretched her arms round it and broke off a bit with each hand. Now, which was which?

She nibbled the right-hand bit and, the next moment, felt a violent blow beneath her chin: it had struck her foot. She was frightened at this, because her chin was pressed so closely against her foot that she could hardly open her mouth; but she did, and swallowed a morsel of the left-hand bit.

"My head's free at last!"

said Alice.

Her delight changed to alarm when she found that her shoulders were nowhere to be found. All she could see was an immense length of neck, rising like a stalk out of the sea of green leaves that lay far below her. She was pleased to find that her neck would bend easily in any direction. She had just curved it down when a sharp hiss made her draw back. A large pigeon had flown into her face.

"Serpent!" screamed the Pigeon.

"I'm not a serpent!" said Alice.

"Serpent!" repeated the Pigeon. "I've tried every way, and nothing suits them. I've tried banks, I've tried hedges, but there's no pleasing them!"

"I haven't the faintest idea what you're talking about," said Alice.

"As if it wasn't trouble enough hatching eggs," said the Pigeon, "but I must be on the look-out for serpents night and day. And now they come wriggling down from the sky. Ugh! Serpent!"

"But I'm not a serpent," said Alice. "I'm a little girl."

"A likely story!" said the Pigeon. "I've never seen a little girl with a neck like that. I suppose you'll tell me next that you've never tasted an egg!"

"I have tasted eggs, certainly," Alice admitted.

"Why then, you're a kind of serpent. Be off!" said the Pigeon sulkily, as it settled into its nest.

Alice crouched down as well as she could, tangled among the branches, and set to work nibbling the pieces of mushroom.

When she was down to her usual height, she walked on and came upon a little house, about four feet high. "Whoever lives there," thought Alice, "I should frighten them out of their wits, at this size." So she nibbled the right-hand bit again, and did not go near the house till she had brought herself down to nine inches high.

CHAPTER 6
Pig and Pepper

For a minute or two, she stood looking at the house. Suddenly a footman came running out of the wood (he looked like a footman because he was in livery, otherwise he looked like a fish) and rapped loudly at the door. It was opened by another footman, with a round face and large eyes like a frog.

The Fish-Footman produced a great letter, nearly as large as himself, and handed it to the other, saying, "For the Duchess. An invitation from the Queen to play croquet."

They both bowed low, and their curls got tangled together.

Alice laughed so much that she had to run back into the wood. When she next peeped out, the Fish-Footman was gone, and the other was staring stupidly up into the sky.

Alice went timidly up to the door and knocked.

"There's no use knocking," said the Footman, "and for two reasons. First, because I'm on the same side of the door as you; secondly, because they're making such a noise inside, no one could possibly hear you."

There certainly was a most extraordinary noise within, a howling and sneezing, and the crashing of dishes.

"How am I to get in, then?" asked Alice.

"Are you to get in at all?" said the Footman.

Just then, the door opened, and a plate came skimming out, grazing the Footman's nose. Alice went right in.

The door led into a kitchen. The Duchess was sitting in the middle, nursing a baby; the cook was stirring a large pot of soup. "There's too much pepper in that soup," Alice said to herself, sneezing.

The only things that did not sneeze were the cook and a large cat, which was sitting on the hearth, grinning from ear to ear.

"Why does your cat grin like that?" said Alice.

"It's a Cheshire cat," said the Duchess.

"I didn't know that Cheshire cats could grin," said Alice.

"All cats can," said the Duchess, "and most of 'em do."

At this point, the cook took the pot of soup off the fire, then set to work throwing things at the Duchess and the baby.

First the fire tongs, then a shower of pots and dishes. The baby was howling, but the Duchess took no notice, even when they hit her.

"Oh, *please* mind what you're doing!" cried Alice anxiously to the cook.

The Duchess began singing a lullaby, giving the child a violent shake at the end of every line:

"Speak roughly to your little boy,
And beat him when he sneezes;
He only does it to annoy,
Because he knows it teases."

Chorus (in which the cook and the baby joined):

"Wow! Wow! Wow!"

While the Duchess sang, she tossed the baby up and down, and the poor little thing howled so that Alice could hardly hear the words:

"I speak severely to my boy,
I beat him when he sneezes;
For he can thoroughly enjoy
The pepper when he pleases!

"Wow! Wow! Wow!"

"Here! You nurse it for a bit," the Duchess said, flinging the baby to Alice. "I must get ready to play croquet with the Queen."

The poor little thing was snorting like a steam engine when she caught it, and kept doubling up and straightening out. Alice looked anxiously into its face. It had a very turned-up nose, more like a snout,  and its eyes were getting extremely small for a baby. Then it grunted so violently that there could be no mistake about it: it was more or less a pig. So she set the little creature down outside, and it trotted away into the wood.

"If it had grown up," she said to herself, "it would have made a dreadfully ugly child. But it makes quite a handsome pig." As Alice was thinking of other children she knew who would do well as pigs, she was startled to see the Cheshire Cat sitting on a bough of a tree a few yards off. The Cat grinned when it saw Alice.

"Cheshire puss," she began timidly. "Which way should I go from here?"

"That depends on where you want to get to," said the Cat.

"I don't much care where – " said Alice.

"Then it doesn't matter which way you go," said the Cat.

" – So long as I get somewhere," Alice added.

"Oh, you're sure to do that," said the Cat.

Alice tried another question. "What sort of people live about here?"

The Cat said, waving its right paw, "In that direction lives a Hatter. And over there," waving the other paw,

"a March Hare. They're both mad. Do you play croquet with the Queen today?"

"I'd like to," said Alice.

"You'll see me there," said the Cat, and vanished. While Alice was still looking at the place where it had been, it suddenly appeared again. "By-the-bye, what became of the baby?"

"It turned into a pig."

"I thought it would," said the Cat, and vanished again. Alice began to walk in the direction in which the March Hare was said to live. When she looked up, there was the Cat again.

"Did you say pig, or fig?" it said.

"I said pig," said Alice.

"Right," said the Cat. This time it vanished quite slowly, beginning with the tail and ending with the grin.

"Well, I've often seen a cat without a grin," thought Alice, "but never a grin without a cat."

She walked on until she came to the house of the March Hare. It had to be the right house, because the chimneys were like ears.

CHAPTER 7
A Mad Tea-party

There was a table set out under a tree, and the March Hare and the Hatter were having tea at it. A Dormouse was sitting between them, fast asleep, and the other two were resting their elbows on it.

The table was large, but the three were all crowded together at one corner.

"No room! No room!"

they cried when they saw Alice.

"There's plenty of room!" said Alice, sitting down in a large arm-chair.

"Have some wine," the March Hare said.

Alice looked all round the table, but there was nothing on it but tea.

"I don't see any wine," she said.

"There isn't any," said the March Hare.

"Then it wasn't very civil of you to offer it," said Alice.

"It wasn't very civil of you to sit down without being invited," said the March Hare.

"Why is a raven like a writing desk?" the Hatter interrupted.

"Riddles. Now we can have some fun!" thought Alice. "I believe I can guess that," she said aloud.

"Do you mean you think you know the answer?" said the March Hare.

"Exactly so," said Alice.

"Then you should say what you mean," the March Hare went on.

"I do," Alice hastily replied. "At least, I mean what I say. That's the same thing."

"It isn't," said the Hatter. "You might just as well say that 'I see what I eat' is the same as 'I eat what I see'. What day of the month is it?"

Alice considered a little, and then said, "The fourth."

The Hatter took his watch out of his pocket and shook it uneasily. "Two days wrong!" he sighed. "I told you butter wouldn't suit the works," he added, looking at the March Hare.

The March Hare took the watch, dipped it into his cup of tea, and looked at it gloomily. "It was the best butter," he said.

"What a funny watch!" Alice remarked. "It tells the day of the month, but not the time!"

"Why should it?" muttered the Hatter. "Does your watch tell you what year it is? Have you guessed the riddle yet?"

"No," Alice replied. "What's the answer?"

"I haven't the slightest idea," said the Hatter.

Alice sighed wearily. "I think you might do something better with the time," she said, "than waste it in asking riddles with no answers."

"If you knew Time as well as I do," said the Hatter, "you would not talk of wasting him. If you kept on good terms with him, he'd do almost anything you liked. For instance, suppose it was nine o'clock in the morning, time for school, you'd only have to whisper to Time, and round goes the clock in a twinkling! Half past one, time for dinner!"

"Is that what you do?" Alice asked.

The Hatter shook his head mournfully. "No. We quarrelled last March – just before he went mad – " (pointing with his teaspoon at the March Hare) " – it was at the great concert given by the Queen of Hearts, and I had to sing

'Twinkle twinkle little bat!
How I wonder what you're at!
Up above the world you fly,
Like a tea-tray in the sky.'"

Here the Dormouse shook itself, and began singing in its sleep, "Twinkle, twinkle... " (They had to pinch it to make it stop.)

"Well, I'd hardly finished the first verse," said the Hatter, "when the Queen bawled out, 'He's murdering the time! Off with his head!' And ever since then, he won't do a thing I ask! It's always six o'clock now."

"Suppose we change the subject," the March Hare interrupted, yawning. "I vote the Dormouse tells us a story. Wake up, Dormouse!" And they pinched it on both sides at once.

The Dormouse slowly opened its eyes.

"Tell us a story!" said the March Hare. "And be quick about it, or you'll be asleep again."

"Once upon a time there were three little sisters," the Dormouse began in a hurry, "and their names were Elsie, Lacie, and Tillie; and they lived at the bottom of a well – "

"What did they live on?" said Alice.

"Treacle!" said the Dormouse, after a moment's thought. "It was a treacle-well."

"There's no such thing!" Alice began.

The Dormouse sulkily remarked, "If you can't be civil, you'd better finish the story yourself."

"No, please go on!" Alice said.

"And so," continued the Dormouse, "these three little sisters were learning to draw."

"What did they draw?" said Alice.

"Treacle!" said the Dormouse.

Alice did not want to offend the Dormouse, so she began cautiously, "How can you draw treacle?"

"You can draw water out of a water-well," said the Hatter, "so you can draw treacle out of a treacle-well – eh, stupid?"

The Dormouse had dozed off by this time; but, on being pinched by the Hatter, it woke up again with a little shriek.

This was more than Alice could bear, so she got up and walked off.

The Dormouse fell asleep instantly, and neither of the others took the least notice of her going. The last time she saw them, they were trying to put the Dormouse into the teapot.

As Alice picked her way through the wood, she noticed a door in one of the trees. "That's curious!" she thought, and in she went.

Once more, she was in the long hall, by the little glass table. She took the golden key and unlocked the door; then she nibbled the mushroom (she had kept a piece in her pocket) until she was about a foot high. Then she walked down the little passage and found herself at last in the beautiful garden, among the bright flowers and the cool fountains.

CHAPTER 8
The Queen's Croquet-ground

A large rose-tree stood near the entrance of the garden. The roses on it were white, but there were three gardeners busily painting them red. Alice heard one of them say, "Look out now, Five! Don't splash paint over me like that!"

"I couldn't help it," said Five, sulkily. "Seven jogged my elbow."

Seven flung down his brush. His eye chanced to fall upon Alice. The others looked also, and all of them bowed.

"Why are you painting those roses?" said Alice timidly.

"The fact is, Miss," Two began in a low voice, "this here ought to have been a red rose-tree, and we put in white by mistake. If the Queen was to find out, we should all have our heads cut off – "

At this moment, Five called out, "The Queen! The Queen!" and the three gardeners threw themselves flat on their faces.

First came ten soldiers carrying clubs. These were oblong and flat, like the gardeners. Next came the courtiers, and then the royal children, jumping along, hand in hand. Next came the guests, mostly Kings and Queens, and among them the White Rabbit, talking nervously and smiling. Then followed the Knave of Hearts, and, last of all, the King and Queen of Hearts.

When the procession came to Alice, they stopped and looked at her, and the Queen said severely, "What's your name, child?"

"Alice, your Majesty," said Alice politely, adding to herself, "Why they're only a pack of cards. I needn't be afraid of them!"

"And who are these?" said the Queen, pointing to the gardeners lying on their faces.

"How should I know?" said Alice.

The Queen turned crimson with fury, and screamed,

"Off with her head!"

"Nonsense!" said Alice loudly, and the Queen was silent.

"Consider, my dear," said the King timidly, "she is only a child."

The Queen turned angrily to the gardeners. "Get up!" she said, in a shrill voice.

The gardeners jumped up and began bowing to everybody.

"Leave off that!" screamed the Queen. "What have you been doing here?"

"Please your Majesty," said Two, going down on one knee, "we – "

"I see!" said the Queen, examining the roses. "Off with their heads!"

The procession moved on, leaving three soldiers behind to execute the unhappy gardeners, who ran to Alice for protection.

Alice put them in a large flower pot. After wandering about looking for them for a minute or two, the soldiers marched off after the others.

"Are their heads off?" shouted the Queen.

"Their heads are gone, your Majesty!" the soldiers shouted in reply.

"Right!" shouted the Queen, turning to Alice. "Can you play croquet?"

"Yes!" shouted Alice.

"Come on then!" roared the Queen, and Alice joined the procession.

She was walking by the White Rabbit, who was peeping anxiously into her face. "Where's the Duchess?" she asked.

"Hush!" whispered the Rabbit. "She's under sentence of execution. She boxed the Queen's ears – "

"Get to your places!" thundered the Queen. People began running in all directions, and the game began.

Alice had
never seen such a curious
croquet-ground in all her life. It was
all ridges and furrows; the balls were live hedgehogs,
the mallets live flamingoes, and the soldiers had to double
themselves up to make the arches. The chief difficulty Alice
found was in managing her flamingo. Just as she was going to
give the hedgehog a blow with its head, it would twist itself
round and look up in her face with such a puzzled expression
that she couldn't help laughing; and when she got its head
down again, the hedgehog had unrolled and crawled away.

The players all played at once, quarrelling, and fighting for
the hedgehogs, and the Queen was stamping about shouting
"Off with his head!" about once a minute.

Alice was looking
for a way of escape, when she noticed
a curious appearance in the air. After a minute
or two, she made it out to be a grin, and she said to herself,
"It's the Cheshire Cat."

"How are you getting on?" said the Cat, as soon as there
was mouth enough to speak with.

"I don't think they play at all fairly," Alice began, when the ears had appeared. "I should have hit the Queen's hedgehog just now, but it ran away when it saw mine coming."

"Who are you talking to?" said the King, coming up to Alice and looking at the Cat's head. The rest of it had not materialised.

"A Cheshire Cat," said Alice.

"I don't like the look of it," said the King. "However, it may kiss my hand."

"I'd rather not," the Cat remarked.

"Don't be impertinent," said the King, "and don't look at me like that!"

"A cat may look at a King," said Alice. "I've read that in a book."

"My dear," the King called to the Queen, "I wish you would have this cat removed."

"Off with her head!"

the Queen said, without looking round.

"I'll fetch the executioner myself," said the King, hurrying off.

Alice went to find her flamingo, who was trying to fly up into a tree, but by the time she had caught it, her hedgehog was engaged in a fight with another. So she went back to her friend the Cheshire Cat, only to find a dispute going on between the King, the Queen and the executioner.

The executioner said that you couldn't cut off a head, unless there was a body to cut it off from.

The King said that anything that had a head could be beheaded.

The Queen said that if something wasn't done soon, she would have everybody executed.

Alice said, "It belongs to the Duchess; you'd better ask her about it."

"Fetch her here," said the Queen. The executioner went off like an arrow.

By the time he had come back with the Duchess, the Cat's head had entirely disappeared; so the King ran wildly up and down looking for it, while the rest of the party went back to the game.

CHAPTER 9
The Mock Turtle's Story

"You can't think how glad I am to see you again, you dear old thing!" said the Duchess, as they walked off together.

Alice was glad to find her in such a pleasant temper, but did not much like her keeping so close to her: first, because the Duchess was very ugly; and secondly, because she was exactly the right height to rest her chin upon Alice's shoulder. "The game seems to be going on rather better now," Alice said.

"'Tis so," said the Duchess, "and the moral of it is – 'Oh, 'tis love, 'tis love, that makes the world go round!' I daresay you're wondering why I don't put my arm round your waist. The reason is, I'm doubtful about the temper of your flamingo. Shall I try?"

"He might bite," Alice replied, not anxious to have the experiment tried.

"True," said the Duchess, "flamingoes and mustard both bite. 'Birds of a feather flock together.'"

"Mustard isn't a bird," Alice remarked.

"Right, as usual," said the Duchess. "How clearly you put things."

"It's a mineral, I think," said Alice.

"Of course it is," said the Duchess.

"Oh, I know!" exclaimed Alice. "It's a vegetable. It doesn't look like one, but it is."

"I quite agree," said the Duchess, but her voice died away. There in front of them stood the Queen, with her arms folded, frowning like a thunderstorm.

"Now I give you fair choice," shouted the Queen, "either you or your head must be off!"

The Duchess was gone in a moment.

"Let's go on with the game," the Queen said to Alice.

The Queen never left off quarrelling, and shouting "Off with their heads!", so that at the end of half an hour all the players except the King, the Queen, and Alice were under sentence of execution. Then the Queen, quite out of breath, said to Alice, "Have you seen the Mock Turtle yet?"

"No," said Alice. "I don't even know what a mock turtle is."

"It's the thing mock turtle soup is made from," said the Queen. "Come on."

As they walked off, Alice heard the King pardon everybody. They soon came upon a Gryphon, lying fast asleep in the sun.

"Up, lazy thing!" said the Queen, "and take this young lady to the Mock Turtle." She walked off, leaving Alice alone with the Gryphon.

The Gryphon rubbed its eyes, and watched the Queen go. "They never executes nobody, you know!" it said with a chuckle. "Come on!"

They had not gone far before they saw the Mock Turtle sitting sadly on a rock, sighing as if his heart would break.

"What is his sorrow?" Alice asked the Gryphon.

"It's all his fancy, he hasn't got no sorrow," the Gryphon answered.

The Mock Turtle looked at them with large eyes full of tears.

"This here young lady," said the Gryphon, "wants to know your history."

"I'll tell her," said the Mock Turtle. "Once... I was a real Turtle." These words were broken by constant sobbing, and followed by a long silence.

Alice nearly said, "Thank you, sir, for your interesting story," but she thought there must be more to come.

"When we were little," the Mock Turtle went on, "we went to school in the sea. The master was an old Turtle. We used to call him Tortoise."

"Why?" said Alice.

"Because he taught us," said the Mock Turtle. "We went to school every day."

"So did I," said Alice. "We learned French and music."

"And washing?" said the Mock Turtle.

"Certainly not!" said Alice.

"Ah! Then yours wasn't a really good school," said the Mock Turtle. "At ours, we had French, music and washing – extra. I didn't need it though, living at the bottom of the sea.

"It's a mineral, I think," said Alice. rithing, and then the
"Of course it is," said the Duchess. straction, Uglification
"Oh, I know!" exclaimed Alice. "It'
look like one, but it is."   Alice said.
"I quite agree," said the Duchess, I suppose?" said the
There in front of them stood the Quee
frowning like a thunderstorm.   nake anything... prettier."
"Now I give you fair choice," s'on, "you must know what
you or your head must be off!"
The Duchess was gone in a nyou do lessons?" said Alice,
"Let's go on with the game,"
The Queen never left off qsaid the Mock Turtle, "nine
with their heads!", so that at th
players except the King, the 'ssons," the Gryphon remarked.
sentence of execution. Then tto day."
said to Alice, "Have you seen tlittle, before saying, "Then the
"No," said Alice. "I dcholiday?"
turtle is."   ie Mock Turtle.
"It's the thing mock turt ask, "What happened on the
Queen. "Come on."   a interrupted, "Tell her about
As they walked off, Alice
They soon came upon a Gr
"Up, lazy thing!" said
lady to the Mock Turtle."
with the Gryphon.
The Gryphon rubb
go. "They never execut
a chuckle. "Come on!"
They had not gor
sitting sadly on a rock
"What is his sorr

CHAPTER 10
The Lobster Quadrille

The Mock Turtle sighed deeply, and with tears running down his cheeks, he went on again.

"You may not have lived much under the sea, and perhaps you were never introduced to a lobster, so you can have no idea what a Lobster Quadrille is."

"No," said Alice. "What sort of a dance is it?"

"First," said the Gryphon, "you form a line along the sea-shore – "

"Two lines!" cried the Mock Turtle. "Seals, turtles, salmon and so on – "

"Each with a lobster as a partner!" cried the Gryphon.

"Of course," the Mock Turtle said. "Advance twice – "

"Change lobsters, and retire," continued the Gryphon.

"Then," the Mock Turtle went on, "you throw the lobsters as far out to sea as you can – "

"Swim after them!" screamed the Gryphon. "Turn a somersault, change lobsters again – "

"Back to land, and that's the first figure!" panted the Mock Turtle. "Would you like to see it?"

"Very much indeed," said Alice.

"We can do without lobsters," said the Gryphon. They began solemnly dancing round and round Alice, every now and then treading on her toes, and waving their paws to mark the time, while the Mock Turtle sang this, very slowly and sadly:

" 'Will you walk a little faster?' said a whiting to a snail,
'There's a porpoise close behind us, and he's treading
     on my tail.
See how eagerly the lobsters and the turtles all advance!
They are waiting on the shingle -
     will you come and join the dance?
   Will you, won't you, will you, won't you,
     will you join the dance?
   Will you, won't you, will you, won't you,
     won't you join the dance?'

'You can really have no notion how delightful it will be,
When they take us up and throw us,
    with the lobsters, out to sea!'
But the snail replied 'Too far, too far!' and
    gave a look askance
Said he thanked the whiting kindly,
    but he would not join the dance.
      Would not, could not, would not, could not,
      would not join the dance.
      Would not, could not, would not, could not,
      could not join the dance.

'What matters it how far we go?' his scaly friend replied.
'There is another shore, you know, upon the other side.
The further off from England the nearer is to France
Then turn not pale, beloved snail, but come and
    join the dance.
    Will you, won't you, will you, won't you,
     will you join the dance?
    Will you, won't you, will you, won't you,
     won't you join the dance?' "

"Thank you," said Alice. "If I'd been the whiting, I'd have said to the porpoise, 'We don't want you with us!' "

"No wise fish would go anywhere without a porpoise," said the Mock Turtle. "Why, if a fish told me he was going on a journey, I'd say, 'With what porpoise?' "

"Don't you mean 'purpose'?" said Alice.

"I mean what I say!" the Mock Turtle replied. "Come, let's hear of your adventures."

So Alice began telling them of her adventures since meeting the White Rabbit. Her listeners were perfectly quiet till she got to the part about repeating 'You are old, Father

William'. Then the Mock Turtle sighed, "I should like to hear her repeat something now," and he looked at the Gryphon.

"Stand up and repeat ''Tis the voice of the sluggard'," the Gryphon ordered.

Alice began, but her head was so full of the Lobster Quadrille that the words came out very queer indeed:

" 'Tis the voice of the Lobster'; I heard him declare,
'You have baked me too brown, I must sugar my hair.'
    As a duck with its eyelids, so he with his nose
Trims his belt and his buttons, and turns out his toes."

"I should like to have it explained," said the Mock Turtle.

"She can't explain it," said the Gryphon hastily.

"But about his toes? How could he turn them out with his nose?"

"Go on with the next verse," said the Gryphon, and Alice dared not disobey.

"I passed by his garden,
      and marked, with one eye,
How the Owl and the Panther
      were sharing a pie – "

"This is the most confusing stuff I ever heard!" interrupted the Mock Turtle.

"Yes, you'd better leave off," said the Gryphon. "Would you like the Mock Turtle to sing you a song?"

"Oh, please!" Alice replied eagerly.

"Hm!" said the Gryphon. "Sing her 'Turtle Soup', will you, old fellow?"

The Mock Turtle, choking with sobs, began:

"Beautiful Soup, so rich and green,
Waiting in a hot tureen!
Who for such dainties would not stoop?
Soup of the evening, beautiful Soup!
Soup of the evening, beautiful Soup!
      Beau – ootiful Soo – oop!
      Beau – ootiful Soo – oop!
Soo – oop of the e – e – evening,
      Beautiful, beautiful Soup!"

"Beautiful Soup! Who cares for fish,
Game, or any other dish?
Who would not give all else for two
pennyworth only of beautiful Soup?
Pennyworth only of beautiful Soup?
        Beau — ootiful Soo — oop!
        Beau — ootiful Soo — oop!

Soo — oop of the e — e — evening,
        Beautiful, beauti— FUL SOUP!"

The Mock Turtle had just begun to repeat the chorus, when a cry of "The trial's beginning!" was heard in the distance.

"Come on!" said the Gryphon, taking Alice by the hand.

"What trial?" Alice panted as they ran, but the Gryphon only ran faster. Faintly, carried on the breeze that followed them, came the melancholy words:

"Soo — oop of the e — e — evening,
Beautiful, beautiful Soup!"

CHAPTER 11
Who Stole the Tarts?

The King and Queen of Hearts were seated on their throne, with a great crowd around them. The Knave was before them in chains, and the White Rabbit stood nearby, with a trumpet in one hand and a parchment in the other. In the middle of the court was a table, with a dish of tarts on it. The judge was the King; he wore his crown over the wig.

The twelve jurors were all writing busily on slates. "What are they doing?" whispered Alice.

"They're putting down their names," the Gryphon replied, "for fear they forget them before the end of the trial."

"Stupid things," Alice began, but stopped, for the jurors were writing 'Stupid things' down on their slates.

"Herald, read the accusation!" said the King.

The White Rabbit blew three blasts on the trumpet, unrolled the parchment, and read as follows:

"THE QUEEN OF HEARTS, SHE MADE SOME TARTS,
   ALL ON A SUMMER'S DAY:
THE KNAVE OF HEARTS, HE STOLE THOSE TARTS,
   AND TOOK THEM QUITE AWAY!"

"Consider your verdict," the King said to the jury.

"Not yet!" the Rabbit interrupted. "There's a great deal to come before that! Call the first witness!"

The first witness was the Hatter. He had a teacup in one hand, and a piece of bread and butter in the other. "I beg your pardon," he said, "but I hadn't finished my tea when I was sent for."

"When did you begin?" said the King.

The Hatter looked at the March Hare. "Fourteenth of March, I think."

"Fifteenth," said the March Hare.

The jurors wrote down the dates and added them up.

"Take off your hat!" said the King to the Hatter.

"It isn't mine," said the Hatter.

"Stolen!" the King exclaimed.

"I have none of my own, I'm a Hatter."

"Give your evidence," said the King, "and don't be nervous, or I'll have you executed on the spot."

At this moment Alice felt a curious sensation.

"I wish you wouldn't squeeze so," said the Dormouse, who was sitting next to her. "I can hardly breathe."

"I can't help it," said Alice meekly. "I'm growing."

"Give your evidence!" the King repeated angrily.

"I'm a poor man, your Majesty," the Hatter began in a trembling voice, "and what with the twinkling of the tea... "

"The twinkling of the what?" said the King.

"It began with the tea," the Hatter replied.

"Of course twinkling begins with a T!" said the King sharply.

"I'm a poor man," the Hatter repeated nervously. "The March Hare said – "

"I didn't!" the March Hare interrupted.

"He denies it," said the King. "Leave out that part."

"Well, the Dormouse said... " the Hatter went on, looking anxiously round to see if he would deny it, too; but the Dormouse was fast asleep.

"What did the Dormouse say?" one of the jury asked.

"That I can't remember," said the Hatter.

"You may go," said the King.

"And just take his head off outside," the Queen added to one of the officers; but the Hatter was out of sight before the officer could get to the door.

The next witness was the Duchess's cook, pepper-box in hand.

"Give your evidence," said the King.

"Shan't!" said the cook.

ALICE'S ADVENTURES IN WONDERLAND

The King frowned. "What are tarts made of?" he said, in a deep voice.

"Pepper, mostly," said the cook.

"Treacle," said a sleepy voice behind her.

"Collar that Dormouse!" the Queen shrieked. "Off with his whiskers!"

For some minutes, the court was in confusion, and by the time it had settled down, the cook had disappeared.

"Never mind!" said the King. "Call the next witness."

Alice watched the White Rabbit as he fumbled over the list, feeling very curious to see what the next witness would be like. Imagine her surprise, when the White Rabbit read out, at the top of his shrill little voice, the name

"Alice!"

CHAPTER 12
Alice's Evidence

"Here!" cried Alice, quite forgetting how large she had grown, and she jumped up, tipping over the jury-box, upsetting all the jurors. "Oh, I beg your pardon!" she exclaimed, picking them up again as quickly as she could. In her haste, she had put a lizard back upside down, and the poor thing was waving its tail about, quite unable to move, until she put it right. "I should think it would be quite as much use one way up as the other," she said to herself.

"What do you know about this business?" the King said to Alice.

"Nothing whatever," said Alice.

"That's very important!" the King said to the jury.

Some of the jury wrote down 'Important', others wrote 'Unimportant'.

The King read out from his book, "Rule Forty-two. All persons more than a mile high to leave the court."

Everybody looked at Alice.

"I'm not a mile high," said Alice.

"You're nearly two miles high!" said the Queen.

"Well, I shan't go," said Alice. "That's not a real rule: you invented it just now."

"It's the oldest rule in the book," said the King.

"Then it ought to be Number One," said Alice.

The King turned pale. "Consider your verdict," he said to the jury.

"There's more evidence," said the White Rabbit, jumping up. "This paper has just been picked up. It's a set of verses."

"Are they in the prisoner's handwriting?" asked one of the jury.

"No, they're not," said the White Rabbit.

"He must have imitated somebody else's hand," said the King.

"Please, your Majesty," said the Knave, "I didn't write it, and there's no name signed at the end."

"If you didn't sign it," said the King, "that makes matters worse."

"That proves his guilt," said the Queen.

"It proves nothing of the sort!" said Alice. "Why, you don't even know what they're about."

"Read them!" said the King.

The White Rabbit put on his spectacles, and this is what he read:

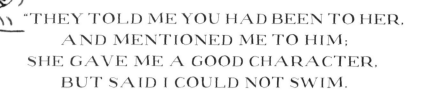

"THEY TOLD ME YOU HAD BEEN TO HER,
    AND MENTIONED ME TO HIM;
SHE GAVE ME A GOOD CHARACTER,
    BUT SAID I COULD NOT SWIM.

HE SENT THEM WORD I HAD NOT GONE,
    (WE KNOW IT TO BE TRUE):
IF SHE SHOULD PUSH THE MATTER ON,
    WHAT WOULD BECOME OF YOU?

I GAVE HER ONE, THEY GAVE HIM TWO,
    YOU GAVE US THREE OR MORE;
THEY ALL RETURNED FROM HIM TO YOU
    THOUGH THEY WERE MINE BEFORE.

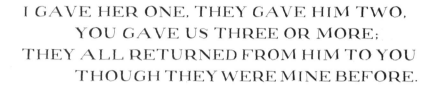

IF I OR SHE SHOULD CHANCE TO BE
    INVOLVED IN THIS AFFAIR,
HE TRUSTS TO YOU TO SET THEM FREE,
    EXACTLY AS WE WERE.

MY NOTION WAS THAT YOU HAVE BEEN
    (BEFORE SHE HAD THIS FIT)
AN OBSTACLE THAT CAME BETWEEN
    HIM, AND OURSELVES, AND IT.

DON'T LET HIM KNOW SHE LIKED THEM BEST,
    FOR THIS MUST EVER BE
A SECRET, KEPT FROM ALL THE REST,
    BETWEEN YOURSELF AND ME."

"That's the most important evidence yet," said the King.

"I don't believe there's an atom of meaning in it," said Alice. (She had grown so large in the last few minutes that she wasn't afraid to say so.)

The King muttered the verses to himself. " 'I gave her one, they gave him two,' why, that must have been what he did with the tarts, you know."

"But it goes on, 'They all returned from him to you'," said Alice.

"Why, there they are!" cried the King, pointing to the tarts on the table. "Let the jury consider their verdict!"

"No, no!" said the Queen. "Sentence first, verdict afterwards."

"Stuff and nonsense!" said Alice loudly.

"Off with her head!" the Queen shouted, but nobody moved.

"Who cares for you?" said Alice. (She had grown to full size by this time.) "You're nothing but a pack of cards!"

At this the whole pack rose up into the air, and came flying down upon her. She tried to beat them off, and found herself lying on the bank, with her head in the lap of her sister, who was gently brushing away some dead leaves that had fluttered down on her face.

"I've had such a curious dream!" said Alice, and she told her sister of all the strange adventures you have just been reading about.

"It was a curious dream, dear," her sister said. "But now it is getting late." So Alice got up, and ran off.

But her sister sat still leaning her head in her hand, watching the setting sun, and thinking of little Alice, till she began dreaming too. The whole place around her became alive with the strange creatures of her little sister's dream.

The long grass rustled, as the White Rabbit hurried by. She could hear the rattle of the teacups as the March Hare and his friends shared their never-ending meal and in the distance, the sobs of the miserable Mock Turtle. So she sat on with closed eyes, and half believed herself in Wonderland, though she knew she only had to open them, and the grass would but be rustling in the wind.

Lastly she pictured to herself how this same little sister of hers would, in the aftertime, be herself a grown woman; and how she would gather about her other little children, and make their eyes bright with many a strange tale of Wonderland of long ago: remembering her own child-life, and the happy summer days.

This paperback edition first published in 2015 by Andersen Press Ltd.
First published in Great Britain in 1993 by Andersen Press Ltd.,
20 Vauxhall Bridge Road, London SW1V 2SA.
Copyright © Tony Ross, 1993.
The rights of Tony Ross to be identified as the author and illustrator of this work have been asserted
by him in accordance with the Copyright, Designs and Patents Act, 1988.
All rights reserved. Printed and bound in China.

1   3   5   7   9   10   8   6   4   2

British Library Cataloguing in Publication Data available.

ISBN 978 1 78344 266 9

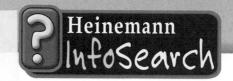

Sweeping Tsunamis

Heinemann
LIBRARY

Louise and Richard Spilsbury

www.heinemann.co.uk/library
Visit our website to find out more information about **Heinemann Library** books.

To order:
 Phone 44 (0) 1865 888066
Send a fax to 44 (0) 1865 314091
 Visit the Heinemann Bookshop at www.heinemann.co.uk/library to browse our catalogue and order online.

First published in Great Britain by Heinemann Library, Halley Court, Jordan Hill, Oxford OX2 8EJ, part of Harcourt Education.
Heinemann is a registered trademark of Harcourt Education Ltd.

Editorial: Andrew Farrow and Dan Nunn
Design: David Poole and Paul Myerscough
Illustrations: Geoff Ward
Picture Research: Rebecca Sodergren and Debra Weatherley
Production: Edward Moore

Originated by Dot Gradations Limited
Printed and bound in China by WKT

ISBN 0 431 17832 1 (hardback)
07 06 05 04 03
10 9 8 7 6 5 4 3 2 1

ISBN 0 431 17860 7 (paperback)
08 07 06 05 04
10 9 8 7 6 5 4 3 2 1

British Library Cataloguing in Publication Data
Spilsbury, Richard, 1963 –
Sweeping tsunamis. – (Awesome forces of nature)
1. Tsunamis – Juvenile literature
I. Title II. Spilsbury, Louise
551.4'7024
A full catalogue record for this book is available from the British Library.

Acknowledgements
The publishers would like to thank the following for permission to reproduce photographs:

Associated Press p. **19**; Corbis pp. **7** (Charles O'Rear), **15** (Todd A. Gipstein), **20** (Bettmann), **22** (David Butow), **27** (Wolfgang Kaehler); Getty Images p. **28**; Honolulu Star-Bulletin p. **12** (Albert Yamauchi); NOAA pp. **4**, **5**, **9** (Pacific Tsunamis Museum), **11**, **14**, **17** (Pacific Tsunamis Museum), **26**; Oxford Scientific Films p. **13** (Mary Plage); Rex Features p. **21**; Scanpix Nordfoto/EPA/AFP p. **18**; Science Photo Library pp. **23** (Carlos Munoz-Yague/LDG/EURELIOS), **25**; Te Papa Tongarewa Museum of New Zealand p. **24**.

Cover photograph reproduced with permission of AGE Fotostock/Imagestate. Unlike in this picture, tsunamis rarely break as they reach the shore.

Every effort has been made to contact copyright holders of any material reproduced in this book. Any omissions will be rectified in subsequent printings if notice is given to the publishers.

Contents

*Any words appearing in the text in bold, **like this**, are explained in the Glossary.*

What is a tsunami?

A tsunami is a huge destructive ocean wave. It is nothing like an ordinary wave. As ocean waves move into shallow water, their narrow foaming tips curl over and 'break' (collapse). A tsunami hits land as a dark, fast-moving ledge of water that rarely breaks as it nears shore. Most tsunamis are barely noticeable in deep parts of oceans, but they get bigger as they approach land.

TSUNAMI FACTS

! The biggest tsunamis are the most destructive waves on the planet.

! The fastest tsunamis in the world can reach speeds of 800 kilometres per hour.

! Tsunamis have reached heights of 40 metres above the normal level of the sea.

There are very few photographs of tsunamis, because people don't usually stand around long enough to take them! This is because big tsunamis may move towards land at hundreds of kilometres per hour. This tsunami was photographed in Hilo, Hawaii in 1946.

Awesome force

Big tsunamis are like huge walls of water. They can be tens of metres tall and several kilometres wide, containing millions of tonnes of water. The water smacks hard onto land with the same force as a wall of concrete.

Anything in the way of a big tsunami – from people to giant ships or lorries – may be swept away, crushed or buried under water. Trees and telegraph poles are snapped like matchsticks. Homes, schools and lighthouses may collapse as if made of cardboard. Over the past 100 years, tsunamis have killed tens of thousands of people and caused millions of pounds' worth of damage around the world.

Harbour waves

'Tsunami' is a Japanese word that means 'harbour wave'. It was given this name because of the great devastation caused around the coastal harbours of Japan by many tsunamis.

Smaller tsunamis may come ashore like a quickly rising tide, gently flooding coastal land. This flooding on Midway Island in 1952 was caused by a tsunami.

What causes a tsunami?

Tsunamis usually happen when giant chunks of land at the bottom of the ocean drop down as the result of an **earthquake**. Millions of tonnes of seawater move in to fill the gap. This causes a series of waves on the surface of the ocean – a bit like the ripples that spread out when you drop a stone into a pond or lake.

Earth movements

The outer layer of the Earth is made of solid rock. On mountain tops it can be bare, on deserts it may be covered with sand, and in oceans it is covered with seawater. Incredibly, this rock is always moving, although it does this very slowly. Deep inside the Earth it is so hot that the rock is melted into a sticky liquid. The cooler, lighter rock of the surface floats around on top of this liquid in enormous chunks called **plates**.

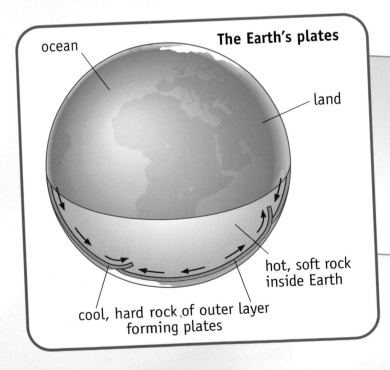

The Earth's plates

ocean

land

hot, soft rock inside Earth

cool, hard rock of outer layer forming plates

As the Earth's plates move, they push and slide against each other. Sometimes the plates stick and then one suddenly slips down, causing an earthquake.

Other causes of tsunamis

All tsunamis start when massive amounts of seawater are suddenly moved. Sometimes the **lava** in the Earth spurts out at gaps or thin spots in the plates. This is what we call a **volcano**. When underwater volcanoes explode, they destroy rocks around them and this can start tsunamis.

Tsunamis can also be started when large amounts of rock or ice on mountains suddenly break free and fall into water. Tsunamis would even happen if a large meteorite (a piece of rock from space) plunged into an ocean.

In 1883, the Krakatoa volcano in Indonesia erupted. The whole island collapsed and caused 35-metre high tsunamis that sped towards neighbouring islands, killing 36,000 people.

Deep beginnings

Tsunamis move outwards from the point where they start. Imagine you are on a plane flying over an ocean. If an earthquake struck hundreds of metres below on the **seafloor**, all you would see is crumpled water for an instant. The sea would then flatten again and a tsunami would speed away.

Tsunamis travel fastest in deep water. The **crest** of a tsunami in deep water may be only one metre tall. This crest is just the tip of a deep wave that reaches tens of metres into the water. As the wave moves towards shallower water, its bottom slows down as it touches the seafloor but the top pushes forward at speed. The water then bunches up and the tsunami is at its tallest as it reaches the coast.

Tsunamis can build to great heights as they get closer to land. Although they slow down, they can still hit coastlines at hundreds of kilometres per hour.

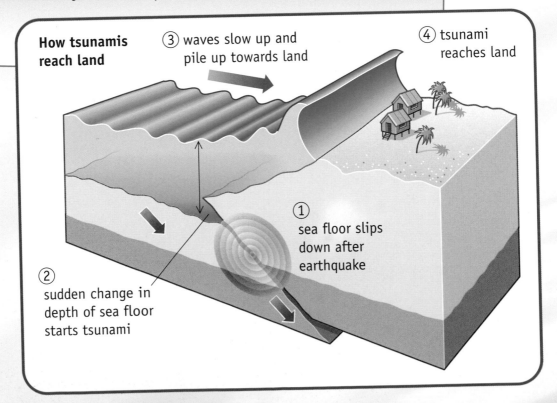

How tsunamis reach land

③ waves slow up and pile up towards land

④ tsunami reaches land

① sea floor slips down after earthquake

② sudden change in depth of sea floor starts tsunami

Enormous forces

Tsunamis shift immense quantities of water at such speed that they can travel over very long distances. In 1960, an earthquake off Chile in South America started a tsunami. The tsunami travelled 15,000 kilometres in 22 hours before hitting the coast of Japan. A big tsunami is barely slowed down when it flows over a small island, but it usually stops after it hits a **continent**. Some large tsunamis bounce back off continents and move back and forth over whole oceans, getting gradually weaker, over several days.

Tsunamis and tidal waves

Tsunamis are sometimes wrongly called tidal waves. Tidal waves are waves caused by tides. Tides are the regular rise and fall of the level of the oceans, caused by the pull of **gravity** of the Moon and the Sun. Especially high tides sometimes cause large tidal waves, but never tsunamis.

Just a few centimetres of moving water can knock over a standing person. Imagine what damage several metres of water, like this tsunami in Hilo, Hawaii in 1946, can do!

Where do tsunamis happen?

Most tsunamis happen in the Pacific Ocean. Some of the countries most at risk from tsunamis are Japan, the USA, Papua New Guinea and Chile, because they border the Pacific. Tsunamis happen here because a part of the Earth's outer surface, called the Pacific **plate**, lies underneath the Pacific Ocean. There are lots of **earthquakes** and **volcanoes** along the edges of this plate, where it meets other plates. This area is often called the 'ring of fire'.

Where else do they happen?

Tsunamis affect other coasts where earthquakes happen in the ocean. They have hit Canada, which is at the edge of the Atlantic Ocean, and Turkey and Greece, which are in the eastern Mediterranean Sea.

The countries around the edge of the Pacific Ocean are all at risk from tsunamis. But certain Pacific islands, such as Hawaii, are at particular risk because they are in the middle of the ring of fire. Tsunamis can approach from all sides!

The Ring of Fire

RUSSIA

Alaska (USA)

CANADA

San Francisco
USA
Los Angeles

•Tokyo
JAPAN

Hawaii
(USA)

PAPUA
NEW
GUINEA

INDONESIA

PACIFIC
OCEAN

AUSTRALIA

CHILE

NEW ZEALAND

KEY
||| ring of fire

Shape of the land

Some parts of coasts are more affected by tsunamis than others. Towns and villages in greatest danger are those at **sea level** less than two kilometres from the sea. Even quite small tsunamis can travel a long way over flat land like this.

Tsunamis are also dangerous in curved bays or at the end of **fjords** (river valleys with steep sides). The waves get very high between their narrow sides. When tsunamis reach **headlands**, which are narrow strips of land sticking out to sea, they wrap around it. Then water floods onto land from both sides.

TSUNAMI FACTS

! The highest tsunami ever recorded happened in Lituya Bay in Alaska in 1958. A **landslide** fell into the narrow fjord, causing a wave over 500 metres high – that's nearly as tall as the CN tower in Canada!

Tsunamis can roll much further inland over a flat coastline like this, than they can over a steep or hilly shore.

What happens in a tsunami?

Tsunamis move very fast. If someone sees one approaching, then it is probably too late for them to get away from it! Sometimes, though, there are signs that a tsunami is on its way.

Many tsunami survivors describe how the **sea level** drops. Water is suddenly sucked away from the shore, uncovering sand, mud and reefs on the sea floor and leaving fish and boats stranded. The reason for this is that the water has moved to fill the space on the ocean floor created by an **earthquake**. Then the water returns in waves.

'It looked as if someone had pulled the plug out from the seabed.' C. Tayfur, a survivor of a tsunami that hit Turkey in 1999.

*Imagine how fascinating it is to see a **coral reef** exposed and fish stranded on the shore. Sadly, many people attracted to a sight like this have been the first to feel the effects of a tsunami.*

Wave train

As the sea gurgles out from land, there is sometimes a very strong wind. This is air being pushed in front of the speeding tsunami. A big tsunami often comes in a series of waves called a wave train. The time between each wave **crest** may be minutes or even as long as an hour. Between each tsunami crest there is a **trough**, when water is again sucked out to sea. It seems like the water is being pulled by an enormous vacuum cleaner before it shoots back!

The first tsunami may not be the worst – the biggest, most dangerous waves in a wave train are often the third and eighth waves to arrive. After the tsunamis have struck, it may take days before normal ocean waves get back to their expected sizes.

The first tsunami wave to break may not cause the most damage. Other, more damaging waves, may arrive later.

Destruction

A big tsunami can destroy almost anything in its path. In an instant, whole areas of homes, farms and factories may be ruined. Many animals and people may be drowned under metres of water, or carried up to a kilometre inland. Cars, trains, boats, buses, shattered buildings and bridges are carried inland at high speed, like missiles. They may crush other things in their way.

The whole of a coastline may be altered by a tsunami. The seawater may flood large areas of low-lying land, ruining farmers' **crops**. Trees, other plants and soil are sometimes stripped from the land, and the sucking action of the wave train may shift whole beaches.

This boat has been carried inland by a tsunami. A tsunami is immensely strong and can move at the speed of a jet plane.

After the waves

When a tsunami is over, daily life does not return to normal for some time. Many people, such as fishermen with broken boats, cannot earn money because they cannot work. Children may not be able to go to school. There are many health hazards. Drinking water and **sewage** get mixed with seawater when pipes are snapped and **reservoirs** broken. People may then drink **polluted** water containing germs that will make them ill. Many are at risk of **electrocution** from damaged **powerlines**. Sometimes gas that leaks from broken pipes explodes.

When the seawater drains away, massive amounts of **debris** left on land have to be cleared up. Some debris comes from collapsed buildings or trees. Other debris is from the ocean – tsunamis pick up tonnes of sand, coral, rock and fish as they approach land.

After a tsunami, there is often a stench from piles of rotting fish dumped on land.

Hawaii, 1946

At around midday on 1 April 1946, an **earthquake** shook the Aleutian Islands of Alaska. A tsunami sped away across the Pacific Ocean. Five hours later, people in the town of Hilo on the eastern side of Hawaii were celebrating April Fool's Day. They were enjoying themselves around the harbour, when suddenly the sea pulled back hundreds of metres. Some walked down onto the seabed to see the **coral reefs** and gasping fish. The 8-metre high **crest** of the first wave caught most people unawares.

*'The wave flipped me over and carried me toward the **lava** rock wall that rimmed the school. I recall telling myself, "I'm going to hit head first into that rock wall and... die." Miraculously, part of the wave that preceded me smashed into the wall and broke it up. So I went flying through the wall... rolling with all the rocks.'* M. Kino, a survivor of the 1946 tsunami

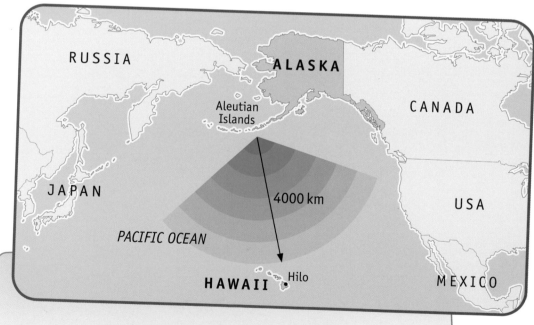

The circles on this map show how the earthquakes that began near the Aleutian Islands caused a tsunami that travelled all the way to Hilo.

Damage

Around 100 people in Hilo were killed by the tsunami and hundreds more were injured. Over a thousand buildings were damaged and the costs of **aid**, clearing up and rebuilding were in the region of US$25 million.

Most people in Hilo had no warning that a tsunami was coming towards them. After Hilo, the US government decided to create a tsunami early warning system around the Pacific. When another big tsunami approached in 1960, warning sirens were sounded and fewer people were killed or injured. Sadly, many of the victims had ignored the warnings they were given and had not moved to a safer place.

TSUNAMI FACTS

! Since 1800 over 40 tsunamis have struck Hawaiian islands.

! Hawaii has about one tsunami a year, and a serious tsunami every seven years.

! Hilo has suffered more tsunami damage than any other US city.

People ran for their lives when the tsunami swept over their homes in Hilo in 1946.

Who helps when tsunamis happen?

Many people help the victims of tsunamis. Scientists tell coast guards and government officials if there has been an **earthquake** that might start a tsunami. Then fire, police and ambulance services, and the navy are put on alert. Hospitals prepare to treat tsunami victims.

Authorities use radio and TV **broadcasts** to warn people that they may have to **evacuate**. They might also visit people where they live to tell them. If a tsunami is definitely on its way, sirens may be sounded so that people know they must evacuate to a safe place. Most people can travel on their own, but some young, old or sick people need help evacuating. The police and army usually help organize evacuations.

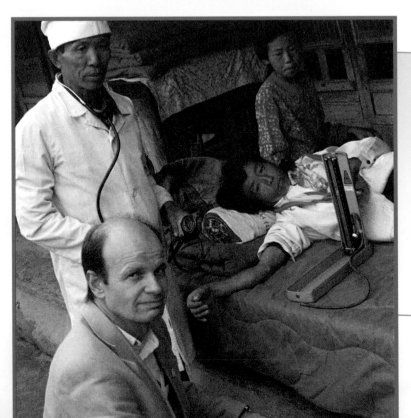

*Local authorities and **charities** such as the Red Cross give **first aid** to injured people. They also collect together food and water supplies and organize shelter for evacuated people.*

Emergency help

More help is needed if a tsunami happens unexpectedly, or if it affects more land than expected. Emergency services find and rescue people washed out to sea or trapped in dangerous places such as boats or unsafe buildings. Fire services put out fires of spilt oil or gas. **Paramedics** and doctors give first aid for injuries such as wounds and broken bones.

In some poorer countries, emergency services may not be able to cope with a tsunami disaster. They will ask for **aid** from other governments and international organizations and charities. Many of these groups may also help over a longer period, working with local people to rebuild homes and hospitals. In places where farms have been destroyed, they give seeds and **livestock** so people can feed themselves again. They also give new pipes and pumps to provide a safe water supply.

This rescue team has landed in a helicopter. They have sniffer dogs to help them find people who may be trapped in collapsed buildings.

What to do when a tsunami happens

- People who live or work on the coast should move two to three kilometres inland or to higher ground.
- People on a boat on deep sea should stay there and not return to land. The height of waves is lower further out to sea, over deep water.
- People should keep a radio or telephone nearby to listen out for further warnings and messages.
- People should never return to a tsunami-hit area until they are told the waves have stopped coming.
- People should keep away from buildings left standing after a tsunami, because they might collapse.

People on boats near coasts should head out to sea if they hear a tsunami warning. Boats near the coast will be tossed and smashed onto the shore like toys, like this boat in Hachinohe, Japan in 1960.

Japan, 1993

On 12 July 1993 an **earthquake** struck 20 kilometres off the island of Okushiri. The Japanese authorities gave a tsunami warning on radio and TV within 5 minutes, so many people were able to **evacuate** to higher ground. However, waves 5 to 30 metres high had already struck Aonae, a fishing village on Okushiri's southern **headland**. Over 200 were killed by the waves.

The Japan Maritime Safety Agency used helicopters, boats and divers to find missing people. Heavy cranes and bulldozers were used to clear **debris** that had filled the harbour.

The sports hall of Aonae Middle School became a temporary shelter for hundreds of people whose homes were destroyed. Their new homes were built further away from the sea, so any future tsunamis would affect them less.

This photograph of Aonae was taken the day after the tsunami in 1993.

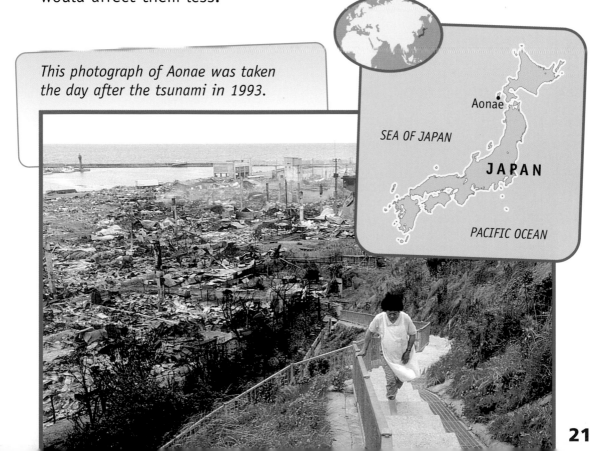

Aonae

SEA OF JAPAN

JAPAN

PACIFIC OCEAN

Can tsunamis be predicted?

Scientists around the world work together to predict tsunamis. They use machines called **seismographs** to record when and where **earthquakes** strike and how strong they are. If a big earthquake happens under or near an ocean, the scientists warn neighbouring countries that it may cause a tsunami. However, not every earthquake starts a tsunami, so scientists have developed ways of detecting and tracking tsunamis.

Detecting waves

There is a network of special research stations around the Pacific Ocean that measure the heights of tides. Scientists use these stations to notice sudden changes in water level that happen before a tsunami. Scientists from Japan and the USA have laid cables on the ocean floor, near their coasts. Special boxes along the cables sense when a deep tsunami wave passes over them. The boxes send this information via **satellites** to scientists onshore, so that they know a tsunami is on its way.

The marks on this paper show earth movements recorded by a seismograph. The more the ground shakes, the bigger an earthquake is.

Looking into the future

Many countries use powerful computers to help them **simulate** how tsunamis will affect their coasts. To do this, they prepare special electronic maps of coastal places, showing where people live, and what the land around is like – for example if it is flat or hilly. They also put in information about previous tsunamis, such as how far they travel on flat land and up steeper slopes. They then simulate different sizes and speeds of tsunamis hitting these places.

Simulations like this are vital to work out the best places to **evacuate** people. Local authorities can then tell people the quickest escape routes if a tsunami approaches. Simulations also show people where the safest places to build are.

These are computer simulations of tsunamis hitting land. They give people a good idea of what might happen if a tsunami were to hit their coast.

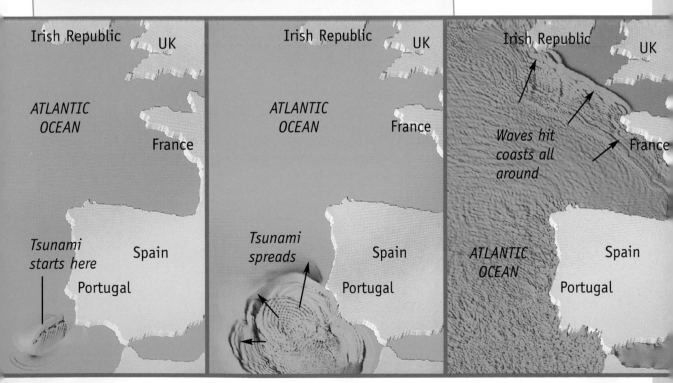

Can people prepare for tsunamis?

People who live in places threatened by tsunamis must understand the danger they are in. They can then prepare in various ways, from the way they build their houses to knowing how to **evacuate**.

Building for tsunamis

The damage caused by tsunamis can be reduced if buildings are made stronger. For example, most of the repair costs after the Aonae tsunami (see page 21) were spent mending damaged harbour walls. Since then new, taller, strengthened sea walls have been built around parts of Japan. In Hawaii, many office and hotel buildings are now designed on stilts – the ground floor is open parking space with rooms above. The water should then pass through the open space and not damage the building structure.

This museum in New Zealand is shaped so that waves can move around it. It is also built on special rubber feet so waves can move it 75 cm without damaging it.

Evacuation plans

It is vital for people to know the best way of getting themselves, their family, pets and farm animals to a safe place. All family members should know how to contact each other or where to meet if they are not all in the same place. They should also know things about where they live and understand evacuation warnings. People should always take evacuation warnings seriously. They should also look out for tsunami signs such as sudden changes in sea level.

A tsunami survival kit

If people have to evacuate, they should take the following:

- a **first-aid** kit and any essential medicines
- enough food and water for at least three days
- a torch and radio with extra batteries
- warm clothing, blankets or sleeping bags
- money and important papers such as passports and their driver's licence.

US states bordering the Pacific Ocean have put up tsunami signs like this, which show people the way they should go if they hear a tsunami warning on the radio or television.

Papua New Guinea, 1998

In July 1998, an **earthquake** started a giant underwater **landslide** that caused an immense tsunami. It was dusk when three huge waves swept over Arop and other villages around Sissano lagoon in northern Papua New Guinea.

Earthquakes are common in Papua New Guinea because it is near the join between two of the Earth's **plates**. However, most of the local people did not know about tsunamis. A rumble was heard out at sea and many people moved closer to see the sea drawing back and then rising above the horizon. Those who could, ran for their lives. The first wave flooded the land and broke up the villagers' flimsy wooden houses. The second wave, which was ten metres high, swept everything away in front of it. Two whole villages were completely destroyed. Thousands of people were injured or killed, many by being thrown against trees or being hit by floating **debris**. Many of the victims were children.

These pictures show a village centre before and after the tsunami of 1998. Whole buildings were wiped out by the tsunami's awesome power.

Future safety

After the disaster, Australian emergency services and **charities** such as Oxfam worked with the government of Papua New Guinea to look after survivors. They provided **aid** and helped them rebuild their lives. They also showed local people what to do if another tsunami happened.

Charity workers and the government of Papua New Guinea produced posters, leaflets, special TV programmes and videos about tsunamis. They took these to all the coastal villages and told local people what to do if a tsunami happens. In November 2000 another, smaller, tsunami struck, but amazingly no-one was killed. Most people had remembered their lessons. They had climbed to high ground as soon as the earth began to shake and the **sea level** changed.

In Papua New Guinea, children are now taught all about tsunamis at school. Teachers explain that Papua New Guinea has been hit by many earthquakes and tsunamis, and tell the children what to do if a tsunami happens.

Can tsunamis be prevented?

Tsunamis are natural events that have happened throughout the history of the Earth. Just as we cannot stop **earthquakes** or **volcanoes**, we cannot prevent tsunamis. There has been at least one tsunami a year in the Pacific Ocean since 1800, and there will be more in future. Big tsunamis that affect the coasts of many countries happen around once every seven to ten years.

Changing world

As the population of the world grows, coastal towns and cities get bigger. This means that each tsunami may affect more people. Some US states have areas of sand and gravel on their coast. These were dropped there by big tsunamis in the past when few people lived there. If a big tsunami happened now, millions of people on the US Pacific coast might be affected.

The key to dealing with tsunamis in future is to be prepared by learning what they are and what to do if one happens.

Destructive tsunamis of the 20th century

1908, Calabria, Italy

After an **earthquake**, a 15-metre high tsunami killed almost 100,000 people.

1933, Sanriku, Japan

An earthquake created a tsunami that killed 3000 people, broke 9000 buildings, and overturned 8000 boats. The waves were felt as far away as Iquique, Chile.

1958, Lituya Bay, Alaska, USA

An earthquake shook 90 million tonnes of icy rock from a **fjord** wall. It caused an enormous tsunami that carried moored boats out to sea and stripped the fjord walls of all their soil and plants.

1960, Hilo, Hawaii, USA

A earthquake in Chile sent 10-metre waves towards many Pacific islands. Waves killed 100 people in Japan. In Hilo, Hawaii, over 200 buildings were destroyed.

1964, Anchorage, Alaska

A tsunami sped along the Pacific coast at more than 600 kilometres an hour, crushing houses. Later it hit Crescent City, California, USA, destroying many more buildings. Waves also hit Japan, 6000 kilometres away.

1979, Irian, Indonesia

Several earthquakes caused a series of tsunamis that destroyed many houses along the coast and killed around 100 people.

1979, Majuro, Marshall Islands

Two sets of tsunamis, a week apart, brought waves almost 7 metres high. They destroyed almost the entire city of Majuro, but no one was killed.

1979, San Juan island, Colombia

250 people were drowned when a tsunami destroyed all the houses on the island.

Glossary

aid help given as money, medicine, food or other essential items

broadcast programme (on radio or TV) that gives information to many people

charity organization that gives out aid and makes people aware of disasters

continent seven large land masses on earth – Asia, Africa, North America, South America, Europe, Australia and Antarctica

coral reef hard substance built by colonies of tiny animals. After many years the coral builds up into a huge bank called a reef.

crest highest point

crop plant grown by people for food or other uses

debris broken pieces of buildings, trees, rocks, etc.

earthquake shaking of the ground caused by large movements inside the Earth

electrocution when someone is injured by electricity

evacuate move away from danger until it is safe to return

first aid first medical help given to injured people

fjord narrow strip of sea between high cliffs

gravity force which attracts objects together and which holds us on the ground

headland strip of land sticking out into the sea

landslide when a large piece of land suddenly slides down a slope

lava melted rock from inside the Earth that comes out of a volcano

livestock animals kept by people to eat or to sell

paramedic medical worker who travels to where an accident has happened to help people

plate sheet of rock that forms part of the surface of the Earth

polluted when air, soil or water is poisoned or dirtied

powerlines cables that carry electricity

reservoir large natural or man-made lake used to collect and store water

satellite object made by humans and put into space. Satellites do jobs such as sending out TV signals or taking photographs.

sea level normal level of the sea's surface and land that is at the same level

seafloor solid bottom of a sea or ocean

seismograph machine that records the force and direction of an earthquake

sewage waste matter from toilets and drains

simulate to show accurately how something would happen

trough a wave's trough is its lowest level

volcano hole in the Earth's surface through which lava, hot gases, smoke and ash escape

Find out more

Books

DK Eyewitness Guides: Discover the Power of Volcanoes and Earthquakes – from Hot Spots and Black Smokers to Devastating Tremors and Tsunamis, Susanna van Rose (Dorling Kindersley, 1992)

Floods and Tidal Waves, Terry Jennings (Belitha Press, 1999)

Websites

www.howstuffworks.com – this website contains a detailed explanation of how earthquakes work.

www.fema.gov/kids/tsunami.htm – this website gives facts about tsunami dangers, including what to do and how to prepare.

www.tsunaml.org – the website of the Pacific Tsunami Museum, which has photos and stories of tsunamis in the past.

Disclaimer

All the Internet addresses (URLs) given in this book were valid at the time of going to press. However, due to the dynamic nature of the Internet, some addresses may have changed, or sites may have changed or ceased to exist since publication. While the author and publishers regret any inconvenience this may cause readers, no responsibility for any such changes can be accepted by either the author or the publishers.

Index